John A. J. Creswell, United States Congress

Oration on the Life and Character of Henry Winter Davis

John A. J. Creswell, United States Congress

Oration on the Life and Character of Henry Winter Davis

ISBN/EAN: 9783337255527

Printed in Europe, USA, Canada, Australia, Japan

Cover: Foto ©Andreas Hilbeck / pixelio.de

More available books at **www.hansebooks.com**

ORATION

ON THE

LIFE AND CHARACTER

OF

HENRY WINTER DAVIS,

BY

HON. JOHN A. J. CRESWELL.

Delivered in the Hall of the House of Representatives,
February 22, 1866.

WASHINGTON:
GOVERNMENT PRINTING OFFICE.
1866.

PREFACE.

The death of Hon. HENRY WINTER DAVIS, for many years a distinguished Representative of one of the Baltimore congressional districts, created a deep sensation among those who had been associated with him in national legislation, and they deemed it fitting to pay to his memory unusual honors. They adopted resolutions expressive of their grief, and invited Hon. JOHN A. J. CRESWELL, a Senator of the United States from the State of Maryland, to deliver an oration on his life and character, in the hall of the House of Representatives, on the 22d of February, a day the recurrence of which ever gives increased warmth to patriotic emotions.

The hall of the House was filled by a distinguished audience to listen to the oration. Before eleven o'clock the galleries were crowded in every part. The flags above the Speaker's desk were draped in black, and other insignia of mourning were exhibited. An excellent portrait of the late Hon. HENRY WINTER DAVIS was visible through the folds of the national banner above the Speaker's chair. As on the occasion of the oration on President LINCOLN by Hon. GEORGE BANCROFT, the Marine band occupied the ante-room of the reporters' gallery, and discoursed appropriate music.

At twelve o'clock the senators entered, and the judges of the Supreme Court, preceded by Chief Justice Chase. Of the Cabinet Secretary Stanton and Secretary McCulloch were present. After prayer by the chaplain, the Declaration of Independence was read by Hon. EDWARD McPHERSON, Clerk of the House. After the reading of the Declaration, followed by the playing of a dirge by the band, Hon. SCHUYLER COLFAX, Speaker of the House of Representatives, introduced the orator of the day, Hon. J. A. J. CRESWELL.

REMARKS

OF

HON. SCHUYLER COLFAX,

SPEAKER OF THE HOUSE OF REPRESENTATIVES.

Hon. SCHUYLER COLFAX, Speaker of the House of Representatives, said:

LADIES AND GENTLEMEN: The duty has been devolved upon me of introducing to you the friend and fellow-member, here, of HENRY WINTER DAVIS, and I shall detain you but a moment from his address, to which you will listen with saddened interest.

The world always appreciates and honors courage: the courage of Christianity, which sustained martys in the amphitheatre, at the stake, and on the rack; the courage of Patriotism, which inspired millions in our own land to realize the historic fable of Curtius, and to fill up with their own bodies, if need be, the yawning chasm which imperiled the republic; the courage of Humanity, which is witnessed in the pest-house and the hospital, at the death-bed of the homeless and the prison-cell of the convict. But there is a courage of Statesmen, besides; and nobly was it illustrated by the statesman whose national services we commemorate to-day. Inflexibly hostile to oppression, whether of slaves on American soil or of republicans struggling in Mexico against monarchical invasion, faithful always to principle and liberty, championing always the cause of the downtrodden, fearless as he was eloquent in his avowals, he was mourned throughout a continent; and from the Patapsco to the Gulf the blessings of those who had been ready to perish followed him to his tomb. It is fitting, therefore, though dying a private citizen, that the nation should render him such marked and unusual honors in this hall, the scene of so many of his intellectual triumphs; and I have great pleasure in introducing to you, as the orator of the day, Hon. J. A. J. CRESWELL, his colleague in the thirty-eighth Congress, and now Senator from the State of Maryland.

ORATION

OF

HON. JOHN A. J. CRESWELL.

My Countrymen: On the 22d day of February, 1732, God gave to the world the highest type of humanity, in the person of George Washington. Combining within himself the better qualities of the soldier, sage, statesman, and patriot, alike brave, wise, discreet, and incorruptible, the common consent of mankind has awarded him the incomparable title of Father of his Country. Among all nations and in every clime the richest treasures of language have been exhausted in the effort to transmit to posterity a faithful record of his deeds. For him unfading laurels are secure, so long as letters shall survive and history shall continue to be the guide and teacher of civilized men. The whole human race has become the self-appointed guardian of his fame, and the name of Washington will be ever held, over all the earth, to be synonymous with the highest perfection attainable in public or private life, and coeternal with that immortal love to which reason and revelation have together toiled to elevate human aspirations—the love of liberty, restrained and guarded by law.

But in the presence of the Omnipotent how insignificant is the proudest and the noblest of men! Even Washington, who alone of his kind could fill that comprehensive epitome of General Henry Lee, so often on our lips, "First in war, first in peace, and first in the hearts of his countrymen," was allowed no exemption from the common lot of mortals. In the sixty-eighth year of his age he, too, paid the debt of nature.

The dread announcement of his demise sped over the land like a pestilence, burdening the very air with mourning, and carrying inexpressible sorrow to every household and every heart. The course of legislation was stopped in mid career to give expression to the grief of Congress, and by resolution, approved January 6, 1800, the 22d of February of that year was devoted to national humiliation and lamentation. This is, then, as well a day of sorrow as a day of rejoicing.

More recent calamities also remind us that death is universal king. Just ten days ago our great historian pronounced in this hall an impartial judgment upon the earthly career of him who, as savior of his country, will be counted as the compeer of Washington. Scarce have the orator's lingering tones been mellowed into silence, scarce has the glowing page whereon his words were traced lost the impress of his passing hand, yet we are again called into the presence of the Inexorable to crown one more illustrious victim with sacrificial flowers. Having taken up his lifeless body, as beautiful as the dead Absalom, and laid it in the tomb with becoming solemnity, we have assembled in the sight of the world to do deserved honor to the name and memory of HENRY WINTER DAVIS, a native of Annapolis, in the State of Maryland, but always proudly claiming to be no less than a citizen of the United States of America.

We have not convened in obedience to any formal

custom, requiring us to assume an empty show of be·
reavement, in order that we may appear respectful to
the departed. We who knew HENRY WINTER DAVIS
are not content to clothe ourselves in the outward garb
of grief, and call the semblance of mourning a fitting
tribute to the gifted orator and statesman, so suddenly
snatched from our midst in the full glory of his mental
and bodily strength. We would do more than "bear
about the mockery of woe." Prompted by a genuine
affection, we desire to ignore all idle and merely con-
ventional ceremonies, and permit our stricken hearts to
speak their spontaneous sorrow.

Here, then, where he sat for eight years as a Representative of the people; where friends have trooped
about him, and admiring crowds have paid homage to
his genius; where grave legislators have yielded themselves willing captives to his eloquence, and his wise
counsel has moulded, in no small degree, the law of a
great nation, let us, in dealing with what he has left us,
verify the saying of Bacon, "Death openeth the good
fame and extinguisheth envy." Remembering that he
was a man of like passions and equally fallible with
ourselves, let us review his life in a spirit of generous
candor, applaud what is good, and try to profit by it;
and if we find aught of ill, let us, so far as justice and
truth will permit, cover it with the vail of charity and
bury it out of sight forever. So may our survivors do
for us.

The subject of this address was born on the 16th of
August, 1817.

His father, Rev. Henry Lyon Davis, of the Protestant

Episcopal church, was president of St. John's College
at Annapolis, Maryland, and rector of St. Ann's parish.
He was of imposing person, and great dignity and force
of character. He was, moreover, a man of genius, and
of varied and profound learning, eminently versed in
mathematics and natural sciences, abounding in class-
ical lore, endowed with a vast memory, and gifted with
a concise, clear, and graceful style; rich and fluent in
conversation, but without the least pretension to oratory
and wholly incapable of *extempore* speaking. He was
removed from the presidency of St. John's by a board
of democratic trustees because of his federal politics;
and, years afterward, he gave his son his only lesson in
politics at the end of a letter, addressed to him when
at Kenyon College, in this laconic sentence: "My son,
beware of the follies of Jacksonism."

His mother was Jane Brown Winter, a woman of
elegant accomplishments and of great sweetness of
disposition and purity of life. It might be truthfully
said of her, that she was an exemplar for all who knew
her. She had only two children, Henry Winter, and
Jane, who married Rev. Edward Syle.

The education of Henry Winter began very early,
at home, under the care of his aunt, Elizabeth Brown
Winter, who entertained the most rigid and exacting
opinions in regard to the training of children, but who
was withal a noble woman. He once playfully said, "I
could read before I was four years old, though much
against my will." When his father was removed from
St. John's, he went to Wilmington, Delaware, but some
time elapsed before he became settled there. Mean-

while, Henry Winter remained with his aunt in Alexandria, Virginia. He afterward went to Wilmington, and was there instructed under his father's supervision. In 1827 his father returned to Maryland and settled in Anne Arundel county.

After reaching Anne Arundel, Henry Winter became so much devoted to out-door life that he gave small promise of scholarly proficiency. He affected the sportsman, and became a devoted disciple of Nimrod; accompanied always by one of his father's slaves he roamed the country with a huge old fowling-piece on his shoulder, burning powder in abundance, but doing little damage otherwise. While here he saw much of slaves and slavery, and what he saw impressed him profoundly, and laid the foundation for those opinions which he so heroically and constantly defended in all his after-life. Referring to this period, he said long afterward, "My familiar association with the slaves while a boy gave me great insight into their feelings and views. They spoke with freedom before a boy what they would have repressed before a man. They were far from indifferent to their condition; they felt wronged and sighed for freedom. They were attached to my father and loved me, yet they habitually spoke of the day when God would deliver them."

He subsequently went to Alexandria, and was sent to school at Howard, near the Theological Seminary, and from Howard he went to Kenyon College, in Ohio, in the fall of 1833.

Kenyon was then in the first year of the presidency of Bishop McIlvaine. It was the centre of vast forests,

broken only by occasional clearings, excepting along
the lines of the National road, and the Ohio river and
its navigable tributaries.   In this wilderness of nature,
but garden of letters, he remained, at first in the gram-
mar school, and then in the college, until the 6th of
September, 1837; when at twenty years of age he
took his degree and diploma, decorated with one of the
honorary orations of his class, on the great day of com-
mencement.   His subject was "Scholastic Philosophy."

At the end of the Freshman year, a change in the
college terms gave him a vacation of three months.   In-
stead of spending it in idleness, as he might have done,
and as most boys would have done, he availed himself
of this interval to pursue and complete the studies of
the Sophomore year, to which he had already given
some attention in his spare moments.   At the opening
of the next session he passed the examination for the
Junior class.   Fortunately I have his own testimony
and opinion as to this exploit, and I give them in his
own language:

"It was a pretty sharp trial of resolution and dogged diligence,
but it saved me a year of college, and indurated my powers of study
and mental culture into a habit, and perhaps enabled me to stay
long enough to graduate.   I do not recommend the example to those
who are independently situated, for learning must fall like the
rain in such gentle showers as to sink in if it is to be fruitful;
when poured on the richest soil in torrents, it not only runs off
without strengthening vegetation, but washes away the soil itself."

His college life was laborious and successful.   The
regular studies were prosecuted with diligence, and from
them he derived great profit, not merely in knowledge,
but in what is of vastly more account, the habit and

power of mental labor. These studies were wrought into his mind and made part of the intellectual substance by the vigorous collisions of the societies in which he delighted. For these mimic conflicts he prepared assiduously, not in writing, but always with a carefully deduced logical analysis and arrangement of the thoughts to be developed in the order of argument, with a brief note of any quotation, or image, or illustration, on the margin at the appropriate place. From that brief he spoke. And this was his only method of preparation for all the great conflicts in which he took part in after life. He never wrote out his speeches beforehand.

Speaking of his feelings at the end of his college life, he sadly said:

"My father's death had embittered the last days of the year 1836, and left me without a counsellor. I knew something of books, nothing of men, and I went forth like Adam among the wild beasts of the unknown wilderness of the world. My father had dedicated me to the ministry, but the day had gone when such dedications determined the lives of young men. Theology as a grave topic of historic and metaphysical investigation I delighted to pursue, but for the ministry I had no calling. I would have been idle if I could, for I had no ambition, but I had no fortune and I could not beg or starve."

All who were acquainted with his temperament can well imagine what a gloomy prospect the future presented to him, when its contemplation wrung from his stoical taciturnity that touching confession.

The truth is, that from the time he entered college he was continually cramped for want of money. The negroes ate everything that was produced on the farm in Anne Arundel, a gastronomic feat which they could easily accomplish, without ever having cause to complain of a surfeit. His aunt, herself in limited circumstances, by a careful husbandry of her means, managed to keep him at college. Kenyon was then a manual-labor institution, and the boys were required to sweep their own rooms, make their own beds and fires, bring their own water, black their own boots, if they ever were blacked, and take an occasional turn at grubbing in the fields or working on the roads. There was no royal road to learning known at Kenyon in those days. Through all this Henry Winter Davis passed, bearing his part manfully; and knowing how heavily he taxed the slender purse of his aunt, he denied himself with such rigor that he succeeded, incredible as it may appear, in bringing his total expenses, including boarding and tuition, within the sum of eighty dollars per annum.

His father left an estate consisting only of some slaves, which were equally apportioned between himself and sister. Frequent applications were made to purchase his slaves, but he never could be induced to sell them, although the proceeds would have enabled him to pursue his studies with ease and comfort. He rather sought and obtained a tutorship, and for two years he devoted to law and letters only the time he could rescue from its drudgery. In a letter, written in April, 1839, replying to the request of a relative who offered to purchase his slave Sallie, subject to the provisions of his father's will, which manumitted her if she would go to Liberia, he said: "But if she is under my control," (he did not know that she had been set to his share,) "I will *not consent to the sale*, though he wishes to purchase her subject to the will." And so Sallie was not sold, and Henry Winter Davis, the tutor, toiled on and waited. He never would hold any of his slaves under his authority, never would accept a cent of their wages, and tendered each and all of them a deed of absolute manumission whenever the law would allow. Tell me, was that man sincere in his opposition to slavery? How many of those who have since charged him with being selfish and reckless in his advocacy of emancipation would have shown equal devotion to principle? Not one; not one. Ah! the man who works and suffers for his opinions' sake places his own flesh and blood in pledge for his integrity.

Notwithstanding his irksome and exacting duties, he kept his eye steadily on the University of Virginia, and read, without assistance, a large part of its course. He delighted especially in the pungent pages of Tacitus and the glowing and brilliant, dignified and elevated epic of the Decline and Fall of the Roman Empire. These were favorites which never lost their charm for him. When recently on a visit at my house, he stated in conversation that he often exercised himself in translating from the former, and in transferring the thoughts of the latter into his own language, and he contended that the task had dispelled the popular error that Gibbon's style is swollen and declamatory; for he alleged that every effort at condensation had proved a failure, and that at the end of his labors the page he had attempted to compress had always expanded to the

eye, when relieved of the weighty and stringent fetters
in which the gigantic genius of Gibbon had bound it.

About this time—the only period when doubts beset
him—he was tempted by a very advantageous offer to
settle in Mississippi. He determined to accept; but
some kind spirit interposed to prevent the despatch of
the final letter, and he remained in Alexandria. At
last his aunt—second mother as she was—sold some
land and dedicated the proceeds to his legal studies.
He arrived at the University of Virginia in October,
1839.

From that moment he entered actively and unremittingly on his course of intellectual training. While
a boy he had become familiar, under the guidance of
his father, with the classics of Addison, Johnson, Swift,
Cowper, and Pope, and he now plunged into the
domain of history. He had begun at Kenyon to make
flanking forays into the fields of historic investigation
which lay so invitingly on each side of the regular
march of his college course. As he acquired more
information and confidence, these forays became more
extensive and profitable. It was then the transition
period from the shallow though graceful pages of
Gillies, Rollin, Russel, and Tytler, and the rabbinical
agglomerations of Shuckford and Prideaux to the
modern school of free, profound, and laborious investigation, which has reared immortal monuments to its
memory in the works of Hallam, Macaulay, Grote,
Bancroft, Prescott, Motley, Niebuhr, Bunsen, Schlosser,
Thiers, and their fellows. But of the last-named none
except Niebuhr's History of Rome and Hallam's Middle

Ages were accessible to him in the backwoods of Ohio. Cousin's Course of the History of Modern Philosophy was just glittering in the horizon, and Gibbon shone alone as the morning star of the day of historic research, which he had heralded so long. The French Revolution he had seen only as presented in Burke's brilliant vituperation and Scott's Tory diatribe. A republican picture of the great republican revolution, the fountain of all that is now tolerable in Europe, had not then been presented on any authentic and comprehensive page.

Not only these, but all historical works of value which the English, French, and German languages can furnish, with an immense amount of other intellectual pabulum, were eagerly gathered, consumed with voracious appetite, and thoroughly digested. Supplied at last with the required means, he braced himself for a systematic curriculum of law, and pursued it with marked constancy and success. While at the university he also took up the German and French languages and mastered them, and he perfected his scholarship in Latin and Greek. Until his death he read all these languages with great facility and accuracy, and he always kept his Greek Testament lying on his table for easy reference.

After a thorough course at the university, Mr. DAVIS entered upon the practice of the law in Alexandria, Virginia. He began his profession without much to cheer him; but he was not the man to abandon a pursuit for lack of courage. His ability and industry attracted attention, and before long he had acquired a respectable practice, which thenceforth protected him from all annoyances of a pecuniary nature. He toiled with unwearied assiduity, never appearing in the trial of a cause without the most elaborate and exhaustive preparation, and soon became known to his professional brethren as a valuable ally and a formidable foe. His natural aptitude for public affairs made itself manifest in due time, and some articles which he prepared on municipal and State politics gave him great reputation. He also published a series of newspaper essays, wherein he dared to question the divinity of slavery; and these, though at the time thought to be not beyond the limits of free discussion, were cited against him long after as evidence that he was a heretic in pro-slavery Virginia and Maryland.

On the 30th of October, 1845, he married Miss Constance T. Gardiner, daughter of William C. Gardiner, Esq., a most accomplished and charming young lady, as beautiful and as fragile as a flower. She lived to gladden his heart for but a few years, and then,

"Like a lily drooping,
 She bowed her head and died."

In 1850 he came to Baltimore, and immediately a high position, professional, social, and political, was awarded him. His forensic efforts at once commanded attention and enforced respect. The young men of most ability and promise gathered about him, and made him the centre of their chosen circle. He became a prominent member of the whig party, and was everywhere known as the brilliant orator and successful con-

trovertist of the Scott campaign of 1852. The whig
party, worn out by its many gallant but unsuccessful
battles, was ultimately gathered to its fathers, and Mr.
DAVIS led off in the American movement. He was
elected successively to the thirty-fourth, thirty-fifth, and
thirty-sixth Congresses by the American party from
the fourth district of Maryland. He supported with
great ability and zeal Mr. Fillmore for the Presidency
in 1856, and in 1860 accepted John Bell as the candidate of his party, though he clearly divined and plainly
announced that the great battle was really between
Abraham Lincoln, as the representative of the national
sentiment on the one hand, and secession and disunion,
in all their shades and phases, on the other. To his
seat in the thirty-eighth Congress he was elected by
the Unconditional Union party.

Since the adjournment of the thirty-eighth Congress
he has been profoundly concerned in the momentous
public questions now pressing for adjustment, and he
did not fail on several fitting occasions to give his views
at length to the public. Nevertheless, he frequently
alluded to his earnest desire to retreat for awhile from
the perplexing annoyances of public life. He had
determined upon a long visit to Europe in the coming
spring, and had almost concluded the purchase of a
delightful country-seat, where he hoped to recruit his
weary brain for years to come from the exhaustless
riches of nature. When the thirty-ninth Congress
met, and he read of his old companions in the work of
legislation again gathering in their halls and committee-
rooms, I think, for at least a day or two, he felt a

longing to be among them. During the second week
of the session he again entered this hall, but only
as a spectator. The greeting he received—so general,
spontaneous, and cordial—from gentlemen on both sides
of the House, touched his heart most sensibly. The
crowd that gathered about him was so great that the
party was obliged to retire to one of the larger ante-
rooms for fear of interrupting the public business. A
delightful interview among old friends was the reward.
He was charmed with his reception, and mentioned it
to me with intense satisfaction. Little did you, gentlemen, then think that between you and a beloved friend
the curtain that shrouds eternity was so soon to be
interposed. His sickness was of about a week's dura-
tion. Until the morning of the day preceding his
death, his friends never doubted his recovery. Later
in the day very unfavorable symptoms appeared, and all
then realized his danger. In the evening his wife
spoke to him of a visit, for one day, which he had
projected, to his old friend, Mrs. S. F. Du Pont, when
he replied, in the last words he ever uttered, "It shows
the folly of making plans even for a day." He con-
tinued to fail rapidly in strength until two o'clock on
the afternoon of Saturday, the 30th of December, when
HENRY WINTER DAVIS, in the forty-ninth year of his
age, appeared before his God. His death confirmed
the opinion of Sir Thomas Browne, who declared,
"Marshaling all the horrors of death, and contemplating
the extremities thereof, I find not anything therein able
to daunt the *courage* of a *man*, much less a *well-resolved*

Christian." He passed away so quietly that no one knew the moment of his departure. His was—

> " A death, life sleep;
> A gentle wafting to immortal life."

Mr. DAVIS left a widow, Mrs. Nancy Davis, a daughter of John B. Morris, Esq., of Baltimore, and two little girls, who were the idols of his heart. He was married a second time on the 26th of January, 1857. His nearest surviving collateral relation is the Hon. David Davis, associate justice of the Supreme Court of the United States, who is his only cousin—german. To all these afflicted hearts may God be most gracious.

Thus has the country lost one of the most able, eloquent, and fearless of its defenders. Called from this life at an age when most men are just beginning to command the respect and confidence of their fellows, he has left, nevertheless, a fame as wide as our vast country. He died nineteen years younger than Washington and eight years younger than Lincoln. At forty-eight years of age Washington had not seen the glories of Yorktown even in a vision, nor had Lincoln dreamed of the presidential chair; and if they had died at that age they would have been comparatively unknown in history. Doubtless God would have raised up other leaders, if they had been wanting, to conduct the great American column, which He has chosen to be the body-guard of human rights and hopes, onward among the nations and the centuries; but in that event the 12th and 22d days of February would not be, as they now are, held sacred in our calendar.

Mr. DAVIS' had gathered into his house the literary treasures of four languages, and had reveled in spirit with the wise men of the ages. He had conned his books as jealously as a miner peering for gold, and had not left a panful of earth unwashed. He had collected the purest ore of truth and the richest gems of thought, until he was able to crown himself with knowledge. Blessed with a felicitous power of analysis and a prodigious memory, he ransacked history, ancient and modern, sacred and profane; science, pure, empirical, and metaphysical; the arts, mechanical and liberal; the professions, law, divinity, and medicine; poetry and the miscellanies of literature; and in all these great departments of human lore he moved as easily as most men do in their particular province. His habit was not only to read but to reread the best of his books frequently, and he was continually supplying himself with better editions of his favorites. In current, playful conversation with friends he quoted right and left, in brief and at length, from the classics, ancient and modern, and from the drama, tragic and comic. In his speeches, on the contrary, he quoted but little, and only when he seemed to run upon a thought already expressed by some one else with singular force and appositeness. He was the best scholar I ever met for his years and active life, and was surpassed by very few, excepting mere book-worms. He has for many years been engaged in collecting extracts from newspapers, containing the leading facts and public documents of the day; but he never commonplaced from books. His thesaurus was his head.

I have but little personal knowledge of Mr. DAVIS as a

lawyer. It was never my good fortune to be associated with him in the trial of a cause; nor have I ever been present when he was so engaged. But at the time of his death he filled a high position at the bar, and was chosen to lead against the most· distinguished of his brethren. On public and constitutional questions, as distinguished from those involving only private rights, he was a host, and in the argument of the cases which grew out of the adoption of the new constitution of Maryland he won golden laurels, and drew extraordinary encomiums even from his opponents in that angry litigation. He was thoroughly read in the decisions of the federal courts, and especially in those declaring and defining constitutional principles.

Possessed of a mind of remarkable power, scope, and activity; with an immense fund of precious information, ready to respond to any call he might make upon it, however sudden; wielding a system of logic formed in the severest school, and tried by long practice; gifted with a rare command of language and an eloquence well nigh superhuman; and withal graced with manners the most accomplished and refined, and a person unusually handsome, graceful, and attractive. Mr. DAVIS entered public life with almost unparalleled personal advantages. Having boldly presented himself before the most rigorous tribunal in the world, he proved himself worthy of its favor and attention. He soon rose to the front rank of debaters, and whenever he addressed the House all sides gave him a delighted audience.

I shall not attempt a review of the topics discussed in the thirty-fourth and thirty-fifth Congresses. The

day was fast coming when contests for the Speakership
and battles over appropriation bills, ay, even the fierce
struggle over Kansas, would sink into insignificance,
and Mr. DAVIS, with that political prescience for which
he was always remarkable, seemed to discern the first
sign of the coming storm. The winds had been long
sown, and now the whirlwind was to be reaped. The
thirty-sixth Congress, which had opened so inauspi-
ciously, and which his vote had saved from becoming a
perpetuated bedlam, met for its second session on the
3d of December, 1860, with the clouds of civil war fast
settling down upon the nation. In the hope that war
might yet be averted, on the fourth day of the session,
the celebrated committee of thirty-three was raised,
with the lamented Corwin, of Ohio, as chairman, and
Mr. DAVIS as the member from Maryland. When the
committee reported, Mr. DAVIS sustained the majority
report in an able speech, in which, after urging every
argument in favor of the report, he boldly proclaimed
his own views, and the duties of his State and country.
In his speech of 7th February, 1861, he said:

"I do not wish to say one word which will exasperate the already
too much inflamed state of the public mind; but I will say that the
Constitution of the United States, and the laws made in pursuance
thereof, *must be enforced;* and they who stand across the path of that
enforcement must either *destroy* the *power* of the *United States,* or
it will *destroy them.*"

For such utterances only a small part of the people
of his State was on that day prepared. Seduced by the
wish, they still believed that the Union could be preserved by fair and mutual concessions. They were on

their knees praying for peace, ignorant that bloody war had already girded on his sword. His language was then deemed too harsh and unconciliatory, and hundreds, I among the number, denounced him in unmeasured terms. Before the expiration of three months events had demonstrated his wisdom and our folly, and other paragraphs from that same speech became the fighting creed of the Union men of Maryland. He further said, on that occasion:

" But, sir, there is one State I can speak for, and that is the State of Maryland. Confident in the strength of this great government to protect every interest, grateful for almost a century of unalloyed blessings, she has fomented no agitation; she has done no act to disturb the public peace; she has rested in the consciousness that if there be wrong the Congress of the United States will remedy it; and that none exists which revolution would not aggravate.

" Mr. Speaker, I am here this day to speak, and I say that I do speak, for the people of Maryland, who are loyal to the United States; and that when my judgment is contested, I appeal to the people for its accuracy, and I am ready to maintain it before them.

" In Maryland we are dull, and cannot comprehend the right of secession. We do not recognize the right to make a revolution by a vote. We do not recognize the right of Maryland to repeal the Constitution of the United States, and if any convention there, called by whatever authority, under whatever auspices, undertake to inaugurate revolution in Maryland, their authority will be resisted and defied in arms on the soil of Maryland, in the name and by the authority of the Constitution of the United States."

In January, 1861, the ensign of the Republic, while covering a mission of mercy, was fired on by traitors. In February Jefferson Davis said, at Stevenson, Alabama, " We will carry war where it is easy to advance, where food for the sword and torch await our armies in the densely populated cities." In March the thirty-

sixth Congress, after vainly passing conciliatory resolutions by the score, among other things recommending
the repeal of all personal liberty bills, declaring that
there was no authority outside of the States where
slavery was recognized to interfere with slaves or slavery
therein, and proposing by two-thirds votes of both houses
an amendment of the Constitution prohibiting any future
amendment giving Congress power over slavery in the
States, adjourned amid general terror and distress.

Abraham Lincoln, having passed through the midst
of his enemies, appeared at Washington in due time
and delivered his inaugural, closing with these memo-
rable words :

"In your hands, my dissatisfied fellow countrymen, and not in
mine, is the momentous issue of civil war. The government will
not assail you.

"You can have no conflict without being yourselves the aggressors.
You can have no oath registered in heaven to destroy the government,
while I shall have the most solemn one to 'preserve, protect, and
defend' it.

"I am loth to close. We are not enemies, but friends. We must
not be enemies. Though passion may have strained, it must not
break, our bonds of affection.

"The mystic chords of memory, stretching from every battle-
field and patriot grave to every living hearth and hearth-stone all over
this broad land, will yet swell the chorus of the Union, when again
touched, as surely as they will be, by the better angels of our nature."

Words which, if human hearts do not harden into
stone, through the long ages yet to come,

"Will plead like angels, trumpet-tongued, against
The deep damnation of his taking off."

The appeal was spurned ; and, in the face of its almost godlike gentleness, they who already gloried in

their anticipated saturnalia of blood inhumanly and falsely stigmatized it as a declaration of war. The long-patient North, slow to anger, in its agony still cried, "My brother; oh, my brother!" It remained for that final, ineradicable infamy of Sumter to arouse the nation to arms! At last, to murder at one blow the hopes we had nursed so tenderly, they impiously dragged in the dust the glorious symbol of our national life and majesty, heaping dishonor upon it, and, like the sneering devil at the crucifixion, crying out, "Come and deliver thyself!" and then no man, with the heart of a man, who loved his country and feared his God, dared longer delay to prepare for that great struggle which was destined to rock the earth.

Poor Maryland! cursed with slavery, doubly cursed with traitors! Mr. Davis had said that Maryland was loyal to the United States, and had pledged himself to maintain that position before the people. The time soon came for him to redeem his pledge. On the morning of the 15th of April the President issued his proclamation calling a special session of Congress, which made an extra election necessary in Maryland. Before the sun of that day had gone down, this card was promulgated:

To the voters of the fourth congressional district of Maryland:

I hereby announce myself as a candidate for the House of Representatives of the 37th Congress of the United States of America, upon the basis of the *unconditional maintenance of the Union.*

Should my fellow-citizens of *like views* manifest their preference for a different candidate on *that basis*, it is not my purpose to embarrass them.

H. WINTER DAVIS.

April 15, 1861.

But dark days were coming for Baltimore. A mob, systematically organized in complicity with the rebels at Richmond and Harper's Ferry, seized and kept in subjection an unsuspecting and unarmed population from the 19th to the 24th of April. For six days murder and treason held joint sway; and at the conclusion of their tragedy of horrid barbarities they gave the farce of holding an election for members of the house of delegates.

To show the spirit that moved Mr. DAVIS under this ordeal, I cite from his letter, written on the 28th, to Hon. William H. Seward, the following:

" I have been trying to collect the persons appointed scattered by the storm, and to compel them to take their offices or to decline.

" I have sought men of undoubted courage and capacity for the places vacated.

" We must show the secessionists that we are not frightened, but are resolved to maintain the government in the exercise of all its functions in Maryland.

" We have organized a guard, who will accompany the officers and hold the public buildings against all the secessionists in Maryland.

" A great reaction has set in. If we *now* act promptly the day is ours and the State is safe."

These matters being adjusted, he immediately took the field for Congress on his platform against Mr. Henry May, conservative Union, and in the face of an opposition which few men have dared to encounter, he carried on, unremittingly from that time until the election on the 13th of June, the most brilliant campaign against open traitors, doubters, and dodgers, that unrivalled eloquence, courage, and activity could achieve. Everywhere, day and night, in sunshine and storm, in the market-houses, at the street corners, and in the public halls, his voice rang out clear, loud, and defiant for the "unconditional maintenance" of the Union. He was defeated, but he sanctified the name of *unconditional union* in the vocabulary of every true Marylander. He gathered but 6,000 votes out of 14,000, yet the result was a triumph which gave him the real fruits of victory; and he exclaimed to a friend, with laudable pride, " With six thousand of the workingmen of Baltimore on my side, won in such a contest, I defy them to take the State out of the Union." Though not elected, he never ceased his efforts. With us it was a struggle for homes, hearths, and lives. He said at Brooklyn :

" You see the conflagration from a distance ; it blisters me at my side. You can survive the integrity of the nation; we in Maryland would live on the side of a gulf, perpetually tending to plunge into its depths. It is for us life and liberty; it is for you greatness, strength, and prosperity."

Nothing appalled him; nothing deterred him. He said, at Baltimore, in 1861 :

" The War Department has been taught by the misfortune at Bull Run, which has broken no power nor any spirit, which bowed no State nor made any heart falter, which was felt as a humiliation that has brought forth wisdom."

He also said, speaking of the rebels, and foretelling his own fate, if they succeeded in Maryland :

" They have inaugurated an era of confiscations, proscriptions, and exiles. Read their acts of greedy confiscation, their law of proscriptions by the thousands. Behold the flying exiles from the unfriendly soil of Virginia, Tennessee, and Missouri."

And so he worked on, never abating one jot of his uncompromising devotion to the Union, like a second

Peter the Hermit, preaching a cause, as he believed, truly represented by insignia as sacred as the Cross, and for which no sacrifice, not even death, was too great.

But his crowning glory was his leadership of the emancipation movement. The rebels, notwithstanding "My Maryland's" bloody welcome at South Mountain and Antietam, claimed that she must belong to their confederacy because of the homogeneousness of her institutions. They contended that the fetters of slavery formed a chain that stretched across the Potomac, and held in bondage not only 87,000 slaves, but 600,000 white people also. Their constant theme was "the deliverance" of Maryland. We resolved to break that last tie, and to take position unalterably on the side of the Union and freedom, and thus to deal the final blow to the cause and support of rebellion. We organized our little band, almost ridiculous from its want of numbers, early in 1863. A Sibley tent would have held our whole army. Our enemies laughed us to scorn, and the politicians would not accept our help on any terms, but denied us as earnestly as Peter denied his Lord. Mr. DAVIS was our acknowledged leader, and it was in the heat and fury of the contest which followed that our hearts were welded into permanent friendship. He was the platform maker, and he announced it in a few lines:

" A hearty support of the entire policy of the national administration, including immediate emancipation by constitutional means."

It was very short, but it covered all the ground. The campaign opened by the publication of an address, written by Mr. DAVIS, to the people of Maryland, which,

I venture to say, is unsurpassed by any state paper published in this age of able state papers for the warmth and vigor of its diction, and the lucidity and conclusiveness of its argumentation. It is a pamphlet of twenty pages, glowing throughout with the unmistakable marks of his genius and patriotism, and closing with these words of stirring cheer:

" We do not doubt the result, and expect, freed from the trammels which now bind her, to see Maryland, at no distant day, rapidly advancing in a course of unexampled prosperity with her sister *free* States of the *undivided* and *indivisible* Republic."

Mr. DAVIS was ubiquitous. He was the life and soul of the whole contest. He arranged the order of battle, dictated the correspondence, wrote the important articles for the newspapers, and addressed all the concerted meetings. In short, neither his voice nor his pen rested in all the time of our travail. He would have no compromise; but rejected all overtures of the enemy short of unconditional surrender. On the Eastern Shore he spoke with irresistible power at Elkton, Easton, Salisbury, and Snow Hill, at each of the three last-named towns with a crowd of wondering "American citizens of African descent" listening to him from afar, and looking upon him as if they believed him to be the seraph Abdiel. His last appointment, in extreme southern Maryland, he filled on Friday, after which, bidding me a cordial God-speed, he descended from the stand, sprang into an open wagon awaiting him, travelled eighty miles through a raw night-air, reached Cambridge by daylight, and then crossed the Chesapeake, sixty miles, in time to close the campaign with one of his ringing speeches in Monument square, Baltimore, on Saturday night. In this, our first contest, we were completely victorious.

But we had yet a weary way before us. The legislature had then to pass a law calling a convention. That law had to be approved by a majority of the people. Members of the convention had then to be elected in all parts of the State, and the Constitution which · they adopted had to be carried by a majority of the popular vote. He allowed himself no reprieve from labor until all this had been accomplished. And when the rest of us, worn out by incessant toil, gladly sought rest, he went before the court of appeals to maintain everything that had been done against all comers, and did so triumphantly.

Let free Maryland never forget the debt of eternal gratitude she owes to HENRY WINTER DAVIS.

If oratory means the power of presenting thoughts by public and sustained speech to an audience in the manner best adapted to win a favorable decision of the question at issue, then Mr. DAVIS assuredly occupied the highest position as an orator. He always held his hearers in rapt attention until he closed, and then they lingered about to discuss with one another what they had heard. I have seen a promiscuous assembly, made up of friends and opponents, remain exposed to a beating rain for two hours rather than forego hearing him. Those who had heard him most frequently were always ready to make the greatest effort to hear him again. Even his bitterest enemies have been known to stand shivering on the street corners for a whole evening, charmed by his marvelous tongue. His stump efforts

never fell below his high standard. He never con-
descended to a mere attempt to amuse. He always
spoke to instruct, to convince, and to persuade through
the higher and better avenues to favor. I never heard
him deliver a speech that was not worthy of being
printed and preserved. As a stump orator he was
unapproachable, in my estimation, and I say that with
a clear recollection of having heard, when a boy, that
wonder of Yankee birth and southern development, S.
S. Prentiss.

Mr. Davis's ripe scholarship promptly tendered to his
thought the happiest illustrations and the most appropriate forms of expression. His brain had become
a teeming cornucopia, whence flowed in exhaustless
profusion the most beautiful flowers and the most sub-
stantial fruits; and yet he never indulged in excessive
ornamentation. His taste was almost austerely chaste.
His style was perspicuous, energetic, concise, and withal
highly elegant. He never loaded his sentences with
meretricious finery, or high-sounding, supernumerary
words. When he did use the jewelry of rhetoric, he
would quietly set a metaphor in his page or throw a
comparison into his speech which would serve to light
up with startling distinctness the collossal proportions
of his argument. Of humor he had none; but his wit
and sarcasm at times would glitter like the brandished
cimeter of Saladin, and, descending, would cut as keenly.
The pathetic he never attempted; but when angered by
a malicious assault his invective was consuming, and his
epithets would wound like pellets of lead. Although

gallant to the graces of expression, he always compelled his rhetoric to act as handmaid to his dialectics.

Style may sometimes be an exotic; but when it is, it is sure to partake more and more, as years increase, of the peculiarities of the soil wherein it is nurtured. But the style of Mr. DAVIS was indigenous and strongly marked by his individuality. Although he doubtless admired, and perhaps imitated, the condensation and dignity of Gibbon, yet it is certain that he carefully avoided the monotonous stateliness and the elaborate and ostentatious art of that most erudite historian. I look in vain for his model in the skeptical Gibbon, the cynical Bolingbroke, or the gorgeous Burke. These were all to him intellectual giants; but giants of false belief and practice. Not even from Tacitus, upon whom he looked with the greatest favor, could he have acquired his burning and impressive diction.

HENRY WINTER DAVIS was a man of faith, and believed in Christ and his fellow-man. His heart and mind were both nourished into their full dimensions under the fostering influences of our free institutions; so that, being reared a freeman, he thought and spake as became a freeman. No other land could have produced such dauntless courage and such heroic devotion to honest conviction in a public man; and even our land has produced but few men of his stamp and ability. His implicit faith in God's eternal justice, and his grand moral courage, imparted to him his proselyting zeal, and gave him that amazing, kindling power which enabled him to light the fires of enthusiasm wherever he touched the public mind.

To show his power in extemporaneous debate, as well as his determined patriotism, I will introduce a passage from his speech of April 11, 1864, delivered in the House of Representatives. You will remember that the end of the rebellion had not then appeared· Grant, with his invincible legions, had not started to execute that greatest military movement of modern times, by which, after months of bloody persistence, hurling themselves continually against what seemed the frowning front of destiny, they finally drove the enemy from his strongholds, made Fortune herself captive, and, binding her to their standards, held her there until the surrender of every rebel in arms closed the war amid the exultant plaudits of men and angels. Our hopes had not then grown into victory, and we looked forward anxiously to the terrible march from the Rappahannock to Richmond. Thinking that perhaps our army stood appalled before the great duty required of it, and that the people might be diverted from their purpose to crush the rebellion when they saw that it could only be accomplished at the cost of an ocean of human blood, a call was made on the floor of the American Congress for a recognition of the southern confederacy. Speaking for the nation, Mr. DAVIS said:

"But, Mr. Speaker, if it be said that a time may come when the question of recognizing the southern confederacy will have to be answered, I admit it. * * * * When the people, exhausted by taxation, weary of sacrifices, drained of blood, betrayed by their rulers, deluded by demagogues into believing that peace is the way to union, and submission the path to victory, shall throw down their arms before the advancing foe; when vast chasms across every State shall make it apparent to every eye, when too late to remedy it, that division from the south is anarchy at the north, and that peace without union is the end of the Republic; *then* the independence of the south will be an accomplished fact, and gentlemen may, without treason to the dead Republic, rise in this migratory house, wherever it may then be in America, and declare themselves for recognizing their masters at the south rather than exterminating them. Until that day, in the name of the American nation; in the name of every house in the land where there is one dead for the holy cause; in the name of those who stand before us in the ranks of battle; in the name of the liberty our ancestors have confided to us, I devote to eternal execration the name of him who shall propose to destroy this blessed land rather than its enemies.

"But until that time arrive it is the judgment of the American people there shall be no compromise; that ruin to ourselves or ruin to the southern rebels are the only alternatives. It is only by resolutions of this kind that nations can rise above great dangers and overcome them in crises like this. It was only by turning France into a camp, resolved that Europe might exterminate but should not subjugate her, that France is the leading empire of Europe to-day. It is by such a resolve that the American people, coercing a reluctant government to draw the sword and stake the national existence on the integrity of the Republic, are now anything but the fragments of a nation before the world, the scorn and hiss of every petty tyrant. It is because the people of the United States, rising to the height of the occasion, dedicated this generation to the sword, and pouring out the blood of their children as of no account, and vowing before high Heaven that there should be no end to this conflict but ruin absolute or absolute triumph, that we now are what we are; that the banner of the Republic, still pointing onward, floats proudly in the face of the enemy; that vast regions are reduced to obedience to the laws, and that a great host in armed array now presses with steady step into the dark regions of the rebellion. It is only by the earnest and abiding resolution of the people that, whatever shall be our fate, it shall be grand as the American nation, worthy of that Republic which first trod the path of empire and made no peace but under the banners of victory, that the American people will survive in history. And that will save us. We shall succeed, and not fail. I have an abiding confidence in the firmness, the patience, the endurance of the American people; and, having vowed to stand in history on the great resolve to accept of nothing but victory or ruin, victory is ours. And if with such heroic resolve we fall, we fall with honor, and transmit the name of liberty, committed to our keeping, untarnished, to go down to future generations. The historian of our decline and fall, contemplating the ruins of the last great Republic, and drawing from its fate lessons of wisdom on the waywardness of men, shall drop a tear as he records with sorrow the vain heroism of that people who dedicated and sacrificed themselves to the cause of freedom, and by their example will keep alive her worship in the hearts of men till happier generations shall learn to walk in her paths. Yes, sir, if we must fall, let our last hours be stained by no weakness. If we must fall, let us stand amid the crash of the falling Republic and be buried in its ruins, so that history may take note that men lived in the middle of the nineteenth century worthy of a better fate, but chastised by God for the sins of their forefathers. Let the ruins of the Republic remain to testify to the latest generations our greatness and our heroism. And let Liberty, crownless and childless, sit upon these ruins, crying aloud in a sad wail to the nations of the world, ' I nursed and brought up children and they have rebelled against me.' "

Mr. DAVIS's most striking characteristics were his devotion to principle and his indomitable courage. There never was a moment when he could be truthfully charged with trimming or insincerity. His views were always clearly avowed and fearlessly maintained. He hated slavery, and he did not attempt to conceal it. He remembered the lessons of his youth, and his heart rebelled against the injustice of the system. His antipathy was deeply grounded in his convictions, and he could not be dissuaded, nor frightened, nor driven from expressing it.

He was not a great captain, nor a mighty ruler; he was only one of the people, but, nevertheless, a hero.

Born under the flag of a nation which claimed for its cardinal principle of government, that all men are created free, yet held in abject slavery four millions of human beings; which erected altars to the living God, yet denied to creatures, formed in the image of God and charged with the custody of immortal souls, the common rights of humanity; he declared that the hateful inconsistency should cease to defile the prayers of Christians and stultify the advocates of freedom. No dreamer was he, no mere theorist, but a worker, and a strong one, who did well the work committed to him. He entered upon his self-imposed task when surrounded by slaves and slave-owners. He stood face to face with the iniquitous superstition, and to their teeth defied its worshipers. To make proselytes he had to conquer prejudices, correct traditions, elevate duty above interest, and induce men who had been the propagandists of slavery to become its destroyers. Think you his work was easy? Count the long years of his unequal strife; gather from the winds, which scattered them, the curses of his foes; suffer under all the annoyances and insults which malice and falsehood can invent, and you will then understand how much of heart and hope, of courage and self-relying zeal, were required to make him what he was, and to qualify him to do what he did. And what did he? When the rough hand of war had stripped off the pretexts which enveloped the rebellion, and it became evident that slavery had struck at the life of the Republic, unmindful of · consequences to himself, he, among the first, arraigned the real traitor and demanded the penalty of

death. The denunciations that fell upon him like a
cloud wrapped him in a mantle of honor, and more
truthfully than the great Roman orator he could have
exclaimed, "*Ego hoc animo semperfui, ut invidiam
virtute partam, gloriam non invidiam putarem.*"
This man, so stern and inflexible in the execution of
a purpose, so rigorous in his demands of other men in
behalf of a principle, so indifferent to preferment and
all base objects of pursuit, had a monitor to whom he
always gave an open ear and a prompt assent. It was
no demon like that which attended Socrates, no witch
like that invoked by Saul, no fiend like that to which
Faust resigned himself A vision of light and life and
beauty flitted ever palpably before him, and wooed him
to the perpetual service of the good and true The
memory of a pious and beloved mother permeated his
whole moral being, and kept warm within him the ten-
derest affection. Hear how he wrote of her:

"My mother was a lady of graceful and simple manners, fair
complexion, blue eyes, and auburn hair, with a rich and exquisite
voice, that still thrills my memory with the echo of its vanished
music. She was highly educated for her day, when Annapolis was
the focus of intellect and fashion for Maryland, and its fruits shone
through her conversation, and colored and completed her natural
eloquence, which my father used to say would have made her an
orator, if it had not been thrown away on a woman. She was the
incarnation of all that is Christian in life and hope, in charity and
thought, ready for every good work, herself the example of all she
taught."

It was the force of her precept and example that
formed the man, and supplied him with his shield and
buckler. His private life was spotless. His habits

were regular and abstemious, and his practice in close
conformity with the Episcopal church, of which he was
a member. He invariably attended divine service on
Sunday, and confined himself for the remainder of the
day to a course of religious reading. If from his father
he drew a courage and a fierce determination before
which his enemies fled in confusion, from his mother
he inherited those milder qualities that won for him
friends as true and devoted as man ever possessed.
Some have said he was hard and dictatorial. They
had seen him only when a high resolve had fired his
breast, and when the gleam of battle had lighted his
countenance. His friends saw deeper, and knew that
beneath the exterior he assumed in his struggles with
the world there beat a heart as pure and unsullied, as
confiding and as gentle, as ever sanctified the domestic
circle, or made loved ones happy. His heart reminded
me of a spring among the hills of the Susquehanna, to
which I often resorted in my youth; around a part of
it we boys had built a stone wall to protect it from out-
rage, while on the side next home we left open a path,
easily traveled by familiar feet, and leading straight to
the sweet and perennial waters within.

He lived to hear the salvos that announced, after
more than two centuries of bondage, the redemption of
his native State. He lived to vote for that grand act of
enfranchisement that wiped from the escutcheon of the
nation the leprous stain of slavery, and to know that the
Constitution of the United States no longer recognized
and protected property in man He lived to witness
the triumph of his country in its desperate struggle

with treason, and to behold all its enemies, either wanderers, like Cain, over the earth, or suppliants for mercy at her feet. He lived to catch the first glimpse of the coming glory of that new era of progress that matchless valor had won through the blood and carnage of a thousand battle-fields. He lived, through all the storm of war, to see, at last, America rejuvenated, rescued from the grasp of despotism, and rise victorious, with her garments purified and her brow radiant with the unsullied light of liberty. He lived to greet the return of "meek-eyed peace," and then he gently laid his head upon her bosom, and breathed out there his noble spirit.

The sword may rust in its scabbard, and so let it; but free men, with free thought and free speech, will wage unceasing war until truth shall be enthroned and sit empress of the world. Would to God that he had been spared to complete a life of three score and ten years, for the sake of his country and posterity. When I think of the good he would have accomplished had he survived for twenty years, I can say, in the language of Fisher Ames, "My heart, penetrated with the remembrance of the man, grows liquid as I speak, and I could pour it out like water."

At the portals of his tomb we may bid farewell to the faithful Christian, in the full assurance that a blessed life awaits him beyond the grave. Serenely and trust-. fully he has passed from our sight and gone down into the dark waters.

> "So sinks the day-star in the ocean bed,
> And yet anon repairs his drooping head,
> And tricks his beams, and with new-spangled ore
> Flames in the forehead of the morning sky."

From this hall, where as scholar, statesman, and orator he shone so brightly, he has disappeared forever. Never again will he, answering to the roll-call from this desk, respond for his country and the rights of man. No more shall we hear his fervid eloquence in the day of imminent peril, invoking us, who hold the mighty power of peace and war, to dedicate ourselves, if need be, to the sword, but to accept no end of the conflict save that of absolute triumph for our country. He has gone to answer the great roll-call above, where the "brazen throat of war" is voiceless in the presence of the Prince of Peace. Let us habitually turn to his recorded words, and gather wisdom as from the testament of a departed sage; and since we were witnesses of his tireless devotion to the cause of human freedom, let us direct that on the monument which loving hearts and willing hands will soon erect over his remains, there shall be deeply engraved the figure of a bursting shackle, as the emblem of the faith in which he lived and died.

For the Christian, scholar, statesman, and orator, all good men are mourners; but what shall I say of that grief which none can share—the grief of sincere friendship?

Oh, my friend! comforted by the belief that you, while living, deemed me worthy to be your companion, and loaded me with the proofs of your esteem, I shall fondly treasure, during my remaining years, the recollection of your smile and counsel. Lost to me is the strong arm whereon I have so often leaned; but in that path which in time past we trod most joyfully together, I shall continue, as God shall give me to see my duty, with unfaltering though perhaps with unskilful steps, right onward to the end.

Admiring his brilliant intellect and varied acquirements, his invincible courage and unswerving fortitude, glorying in his good works and fair renown, but, more than all, *loving the man*, I shall endeavor to assuage the bitterness of grief by applying to him those words of proud, though tearful, satisfaction, from which the faithful Tacitus drew consolation for the loss of that noble Roman whom he delighted to honor:

"Quidquid ex Agricola amavimus, quidquid mirati sumus, manet mansurumque est, in animis hominum, in æternitate temporum, fama rerum."

www.ingramcontent.com/pod-product-compliance
Lightning Source LLC
Chambersburg PA
CBHW030911260626
47169CB00008B/2802